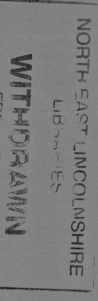

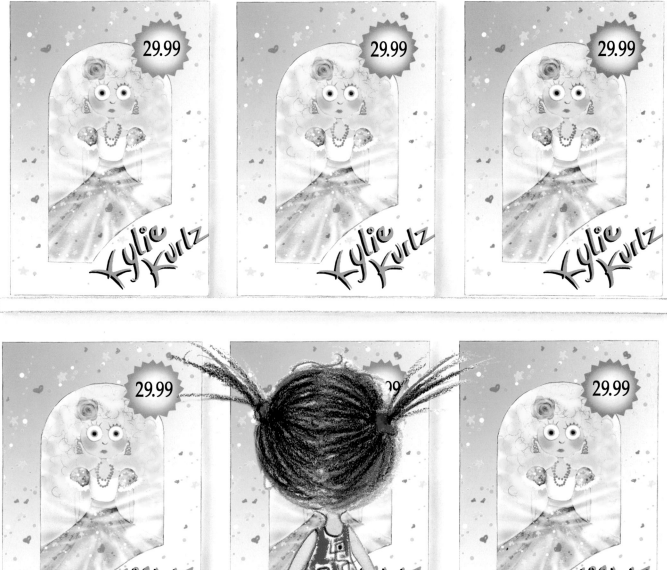

First published 2011 by Macmillan Children's Books
a division of Macmillan Publishers Limited
20 New Wharf Road, London N1 9RR
Basingstoke and Oxford. Associated companies throughout the world
www.panmacmillan.com
ISBN: 978-0-230-75055-5
Text and illustrations copyright © Chloe and Mick Inkpen 2011
Moral rights asserted. All rights reserved.
1 3 5 7 9 8 6 4 2
A CIP catalogue record for this book is available from the British Library.
Printed in China

Zoe's Christmas

List

Zoe and Beans

Chloë & Mick Inkpen

MACMILLAN CHILDREN'S BOOKS

Zoe decided that this year she didn't want Father Christmas to surprise her with a present.

So she made a list.

Zoe's list had only one thing on it.

She knew **exactly** what she wanted...

...Kylie Kurlz.

Zoe decided to go to
the Arctic and stick her
Christmas List to the North
Pole, where Father Christmas
would be sure to find it.

She packed her things.
Choccy Bears (for Beans)
Some juice
2 ham sandwiches
2 jam sandwiches
A scarf
    Mittens
        Some sticky tape. . .

. . . and her Christmas List.

It was a very long way to the North Pole.
They went
on buses
and trains
and boats
and planes. . .

. . . but there were
no buses or trains,
or boats, or planes
that went all the
way there.

So Zoe climbed
on Beans' back and
he swam.

Soon little icebergs began to float past.
Then bigger ones. And bigger still.
'We're nearly there!' said Zoe.

A baby polar bear floated by.
He seemed lost.

'Come with us!' said Zoe.

So the little bear climbed on Beans' back and Zoe fed him Choccy Bears while she told him all about Kylie Kurls and her Christmas List.

'We're going to the North Pole,' said Zoe.

'Woof,' said Beans as his feet touched land.

The Arctic was a wonderful place to whizz downhill on a lunchbox, wheeeeeeeeeeeeeeeeeeeee again, wheeeeeeeeeeeeeeeeeeeeeeeeeeeeeeeeeeeeeeeeeeeeeeeeeeeeeeeeeeeeeeeeeee and over

So that is what they did, over

eeeeeeeeeee

eeeeeeeeeeeeeeeeeeeeeeeeeeeeeeeeeeeeeeeeeeeeeeeeeeeeeeeeeeeeeeeeee . . .

eeee crash!

'We'd better get going,' said Zoe. 'It's beginning to snow!'

The North Pole was further than it looked. By the time they arrived the wind was sending snowflakes spinning round their ears.

It's very tricky sticking
something with sticky tape
in the middle of a snowstorm
wearing mittens.
    And did you know that
when sticky tape gets wet
it loses all its stick. . .

... and comes undone!

Oh No!
No Kylie Kurlz for Christmas

'Let's go home'
said Zoe.

But the blizzard blew
itself into their faces, and
soon they lost their way in
the deepening snow.

Zoe put one of her
mittens on Beans' nose to
keep it warm, and sang
a song about a red-nosed
reindog to cheer herself up.

But the wind just blew
harder and night
began to fall.

As it grew dark the ground seemed to shake. The land began to rumble. And great creaks and groans filled the air! The ice beneath their feet seemed to move . . .

Creak!

As the blizzard howled around them, they curled up together in the snow and fell fast asleep.

Creak!

Crac

In the morning
Zoe and Beans found
themselves floating
out to sea on their
very own iceberg!

The storm was gone.
But so was the little bear.
'Little Bear!
Little Bear!' called Zoe.

'Hello, Little Bear!'

'Look! There he is!'

'Fetch him Beans!'

Splish! Splash! Splish! Splash!

'Swim, Little Bear! Swim!'

(It was at this moment
that Zoe realised
that she wasn't really
all that bothered
about Kylie Kurlz.)

'Ham? Or jam?' said Zoe.
The Little Bear took both.

As they floated away the
Northern Lights came out to play.
'We'll be home soon,' said Zoe.
'But for now let's have
some fun!'

The little bear
pointed up at the sky.

'Look Beans!'
said Zoe 'It must be
Christmas
Eve!'

As they waved to
Father Christmas
Zoe decided that perhaps
it was best after all to
let him surprise her
with a present.

'I wonder what it will be,' she thought . . .

zoe!

Kylie Kurlz &
Kurly Karl
Special
Edition!

Kylie Kurlz